HOP INTO BED!

Nicholas Oldland

North Winds Press
An Imprint of Scholastic Canada Ltd.

Art was created in Photoshop and drawn with the use of a Wacom tablet.

Library and Archives Canada Cataloguing in Publication
Oldland, Nicholas, 1972-, author, illustrator
        Hop into bed! / Nicholas Oldland.

ISBN 978-1-4431-5726-1 (hardcover)

        I. Title.

PS8629.L46H67 2018   jC813'.6   C2017-905172-5

www.scholastic.ca

6 5 4 3 2 1   Printed in Malaysia 108   18 19 20 21 22

To Alice Oldland (Mom), whose
artwork inspired this book.

Bob loved to hop.

He also liked to . . .

fly!

flip!

twist!

bounce!

jump!

leap!

spring!

flop!

and crash!

TIME TO COME HOME, BOBBY!

Bob was in the middle of practising a flying backflip when he spotted his mom and sister.

He landed his flip,

swam . . .

. . . and swung,

. . . ran

all the way home.

Bob flew up the stairs.

He brushed his teeth,

washed his face,

put on his pyjamas.

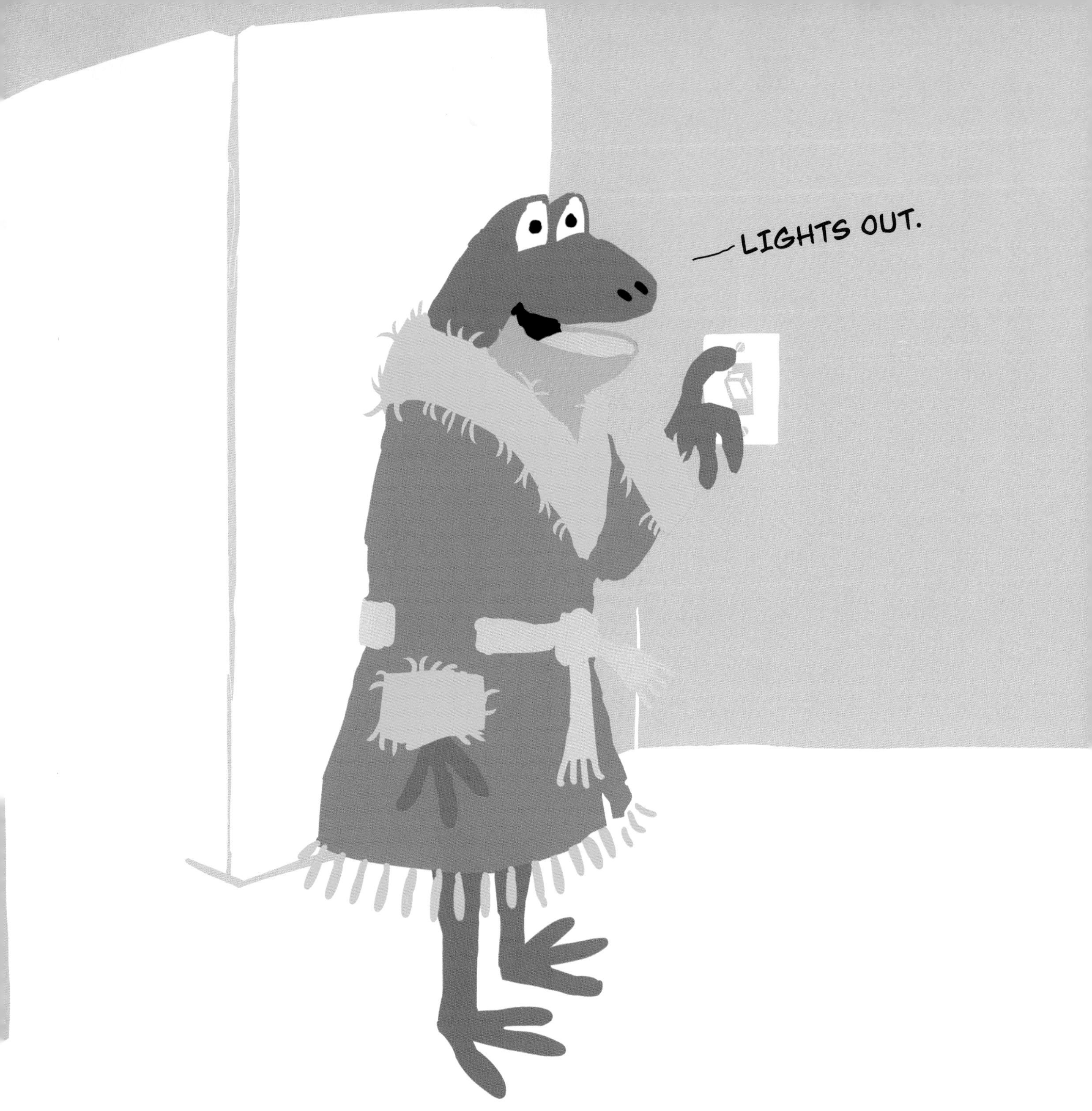
—LIGHTS OUT.

And hopped into bed.

And hop.

But Bob wasn't tired.

All he wanted to do was hop.

And hop.

But Bob kept on hopping. He hopped
until the sun came up.

And then he fell asleep.

Bob's dad tried to get him up.

But Bob could not open his eyes.

So his mom took him down the hall.

She ran him a cold bath.

But he still did not wake up.

His mom brought him
downstairs.

His dad fed him breakfast,
and drove him to school.

But Bob still did not wake up.

At school, Bob slept through English.

He snored through band practice.

Zzzzzz

He even snoozed through a field trip to the zoo.

And he was still asleep when his dad picked him up at the end of the day.

At home, Bob's mom and dad talked to
him about the importance of a good
night's sleep.

After dinner, they told him
to hop into bed.

As soon as he heard the word hop,
Bob shot right up.

He ran up the stairs,

put on his pyjamas . . .

and leapt into
the air.

And with a triple-flip and a
double-twist, Bob hopped.

Right into bed.

And he fell fast asleep.